Discovery

Great British Writers

英國著名作家

Derek Sellen

Editors: Joanna Burgess, Daniela Penzavalle
Design and art direction: Nadia Maestri
Computer graphics: Tiziana Pesce
Picture research: Laura Lagomarsino

Picture credits
Cideb archive; © Bob Masters / Alamy: 5; De Agostini Picture Library : 6, 15, 17, 19, 20, 24, 27, 30, 31 top, 39 bottom, 43, 50, 62, 68, 74, 77, 87, 90, 91; © Robbie Jack / Corbis: 11; The National Portrait Gallery, London: 12 top, 46, 57; © Lessing Archive / Contrasto: 23; © Walker Art Gallery, National Museums Liverpool / The Bridgeman Art Library: 26; © Philippa Lewis; Edifice / CORBIS: 38; © Patrick Ward / Alamy: 39 top; © Leslie Garland Picture Library / Alamy: 40; © Christie's Images / CORBIS: 42; Aquarius Collection : 45, 48; ROCHESTER FILM LTD. / Album: 47; © Neil McAllister / Alamy: 52; © Christopher Wood Gallery, London, UK / The Bridgeman Art Library: 56; The Library of Congress Prints & Photographs Division Washington, DC: 67; The Gallery at Lissadell, Sligo, Ireland, photo Pamela Cassidy: 69; © Bettmann / CORBIS: 71; © Douglas Peebles / Corbis: 76; © Dave G. Houser / Corbis: 78; COLUMBIA PICTURES / Album: 79; © CORBIS SYGMA: 82; UNIVERSAL PICTURES / BAILEY, ALEX / Album: 83, 84 top; Album: 84 bottom, 85; 20TH CENTURY FOX / Album: 86; UMBRELLA / ROSEMBLUM / VIRGIN FILMS / Album: 89.

書　　名：*Great British Writers* 英國著名作家
作　　者：Derek Sellen
責任編輯：黃家麗　　王朴真
封面設計：張毅
出　　版：商務印書館 (香港) 有限公司
　　　　　香港筲箕灣耀興道 3 號東滙廣場 8 樓
　　　　　http://www.commercialpress.com.hk
發　　行：香港聯合書刊物流有限公司
　　　　　香港新界大埔汀麗路 36 號中華商務印刷大廈 3 字樓
印　　刷：中華商務彩色印刷有限公司
　　　　　香港新界大埔汀麗路 36 號中華商務印刷大廈 14 字樓
版　　次：2013 年 6 月第 1 版第 1 次印刷
　　　　　© 2013 商務印書館 (香港) 有限公司
　　　　　ISBN 978 962 07 1993 6
　　　　　Printed in Hong Kong

Contents

The text is recorded in full.

These symbols indicate the beginning and end of the passages
linked to the listening activities. 標誌表示與聽力練習有關的錄音片段開始和結束。

Before you read

1 Vocabulary

You are going to read about the theatre and writers. Match the words A-F with the meanings 1-6. Use a dictionary to help you.

A	stage	C	dramatist	E	sonnet
B	to perform	D	printing	F	imagination

1 ☐ to show a play in the theatre
2 ☐ a person who writes plays
3 ☐ the place in the theatre where the actors are
4 ☐ a way of putting words on the pages of books
5 ☐ using your mind to 'see' things; you need this when you read a book
6 ☐ a special type of poem with 14 lines

2 You will also read about the bad things that some people did. Write the letters A-I in the spaces in sentences 1-5. Use a dictionary to help you. There is an example (0).

A	stole (past form of to steal)	B	spy	F	arrested
		C	stabbed	G	spymaster
		D	crime	H	tortured
		E	murdered	I	war

0 James Bond is a secret agent who works for the government. 'M' is his boss and tells him what to do. He is a ..B... . 'M' is a ..H... .

1 He killed John and took his money. = He .... John and .... his money.

2 He did a very bad thing. The police took him to the police station. = This was a serious .... The police .... him.

3 She killed him with a knife. = She .... him.

4 They did bad things to hurt him and get information from him. = They .... him.

5 When two or more countries fight, there is a ....

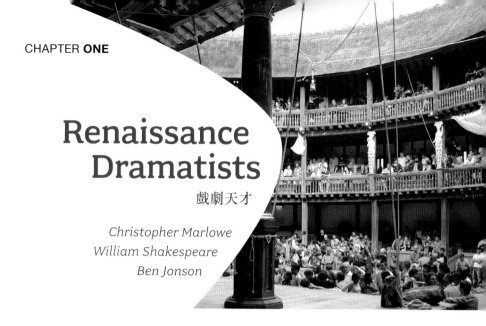

CHAPTER ONE

Renaissance Dramatists

戲劇天才

Christopher Marlowe
William Shakespeare
Ben Jonson

The Renaissance in England

The fifteenth and sixteenth centuries were very exciting times. All over Europe, new ideas were developing. People started printing books and so people could learn more. New lands were discovered. The English language grew and there were new words and new ideas. Theatre was the most popular kind of entertainment.

An Elizabethan James Bond?

Christopher Marlowe was born in Canterbury, Kent, in 1564. His father was a shoemaker but Christopher went to the King's School in Canterbury and then to Corpus Christi College in Cambridge.

Many people believe that Marlowe was a **spy** for the secret service of Queen Elizabeth I. When he was at Cambridge University, he went away for many weeks and no one knew where he was. When he returned, they didn't want to accept him back. But he was allowed to continue his studies because the government spoke to the university. Why? Marlowe was a friend of Sir Francis Walsingham, who was the queen's **spymaster**[1]. Was Marlowe an Elizabethan James Bond?

Living dangerously

Marlowe left Cambridge in 1587 and went to London. He wanted to write plays for the new theatres there. Marlowe soon became well-known in London. He had a social life, went drinking and wore expensive clothes. But above all, he began to write poetry and plays.

His most famous play is *Doctor Faustus*. It is a play about a man, Faustus, who agrees to do what the Devil wants. Mephistopheles, a servant of the Devil, teaches Faustus to do magic. But his use of magic is dangerous and, at the end of the play, Faustus goes to Hell[2].

Marlowe was often in trouble. He went to prison for two weeks because they said he **murdered** someone. Did he go to meetings of 'The School of Night'? This, people said, was a group of writers and famous men who talked about dangerous things, like: Was there a God? Was the Bible true? How could you do magic?

However, Marlowe continued to write plays and poetry. Maybe the government looked after him because he was a good spy. But in 1593, his life became even more dangerous. Richard Baines was an enemy of Marlowe and he told the government that Marlowe didn't believe in God. This was a **crime** in the sixteenth century.

---

1. **a spymaster** : 間諜首領
2. **Hell** : 地獄

Interior of an Inn (17th century) by Adriaen van Ostade.

Next, the government **arrested** Thomas Kyd, another **dramatist** who lived with Marlowe. They found papers with illegal ideas in Kyd's room but he said they belonged to Marlowe. They **tortured** [1] Kyd and he told them that Marlowe didn't believe in the Bible or in God.

A week later, Marlowe died.

The death of Marlowe

This is what probably happened. Marlowe went with some friends to an inn [2] in Deptford, an area of London near the Thames. After dinner, they disagreed about paying the bill. Marlowe and one of the men, Ingram Frizer, had a fight. Perhaps Marlowe himself started the fight. Frizer **stabbed** [3] Marlowe in the face above the eye and the writer died. The government tried to understand what

1. **tortured** : 折磨
2. **an inn** : 旅館
3. **stabbed** : 刺

happened, but Frizer didn't go to prison.

Was it murder? Was it an accident? The other men at the inn had connections with Sir Thomas Walsingham, the son of Queen Elizabeth's spymaster. Did they kill Marlowe for a secret reason?

The last question is this: did Marlowe really die? Some people believe that Marlowe left England because the government wanted to arrest him. Did Marlowe get on a ship and go to another country? Did his friends say that the dead body of another man was Christopher Marlowe? Some people even say that Marlowe went to Italy and continued writing plays there. Then he sent these plays to England and used Shakespeare's name. These people believe that Marlowe was really the writer of William Shakespeare's plays.

From Marlowe to Shakespeare

William Shakespeare was born in the same year as Christopher Marlowe, 1564. He was born in Stratford-upon-Avon in the middle of England. He went to the grammar school[1] in Stratford but he didn't go to university. When he was only 18 years old, he married Anne Hathaway, who was 26. They had three children, Susanna, Hamnet and Judith, but Hamnet died when he was a child.

Why did Shakespeare leave Stratford and go to London? Nobody knows, but

1.   **grammar school**：文法學校

The Globe Theatre today.

people say that he **stole** a deer [1] from a rich man and so he had to leave. When he was in London, perhaps he began his life in the theatre by looking after rich people's horses while they watched the plays. But soon he began to write plays himself for the theatres of London. Not everybody liked Shakespeare. Robert Greene, another writer, said that Shakespeare was a new, young writer who copied other people's plays.

'All the world's a stage' [2]

By 1592, Shakespeare's plays were well-known and popular. He was a member of a group of actors who **performed** at The Theatre and The Curtain, two theatres north of the Thames. But when the actors disagreed with the owner in 1598, they stole the wood from The Theatre and carried it across the Thames. Here, south of the Thames, they used it to build a new theatre. They called it The

1. deer :

2. **'All the world's a stage'** : 世界是個舞台

Globe because the theatre can represent lots of different places in the world. Also, the theatre building was round.

In theatres in Shakespeare's time, some people sat down to watch the play but the people with less money had to stand in an open space in front of the **stage**. When it rained, they got wet. The actors didn't have modern technology [1] like we do in theatres and cinemas now, but they found ways to help the people to imagine Italian cities or ancient Rome or Denmark or Greece on the stage. The people had to use their **imagination** when they watched the actors. Women didn't perform in the theatre in Marlowe and Shakespeare's time, so boys acted the parts of girls or women such as Juliet, Cleopatra and Desdemona.

The main actors were famous like film stars are today. Everyone, from the Queen or King to ordinary people, wanted to see their plays. After James I became king, Shakespeare's actors were called The King's Men. They performed at The Globe in the summer and inside in the winter at Blackfriars in London.

When he began writing plays, Shakespeare usually wrote comedies and history plays. He also wrote a Romantic tragedy [2] that is one of the most famous plays in the world — *Romeo and Juliet*. Most people think that his tragedies like *Hamlet* and *King Lear* are his best plays. His last plays have happy endings and include *The Tempest* and *The Winter's Tale*.

In 1609, Shakespeare published his **sonnets** [3]. Many of these 154 poems are about love. Some of the sonnets speak to a 'dark lady'. Who was she? Are these poems about Shakespeare's life or not? We don't know.

1. **technology** : 技術
2. **tragedy** : 悲劇
3. **sonnets** : 十四行詩

'Our little life is rounded with a sleep' [1]

Shakespeare became a rich man when he was older. He lived in a good part of London and bought houses in Stratford and London. He died on 23 April 1616. Many people think that he was also born on 23 April, which is the national day of England, St George's Day.

Shakespeare's plays didn't die with him. While he lived, he didn't publish his plays. But in 1623, some friends published thirty-six of his plays in one book. Theatres all over the world still perform these plays today and there are many films of Shakespeare's plays.

The Merry Wives of Windsor (2008) at Shakespeare Globe Theatre in London.

1. **'our little life is rounded with a sleep'**：我們短暫的一生，生前死後都在沉睡。

Ben Jonson: 'kind and angry'

Another dramatist who lived at the same time as Marlowe and Shakespeare was Ben Jonson. He joined the army and was a soldier for several years in the Netherlands. He enjoyed fighting. When he returned to England, he married Ann Lewis but their marriage was not happy.

In 1597 he became an actor and a writer. But he went to prison because he wrote something which the government didn't like. The next year, Jonson killed another actor in a fight. He went to prison again, but only for a short time. He went to prison for a third time in 1603!

Later, Jonson took part in the '**War** of the Theatres'. This was a war with pen and paper. Jonson wrote plays which laughed at other writers and they did the same.

In 1618, Jonson walked from London to Scotland. He wanted to visit the area his family came from. Someone who met him in Scotland wrote that he was 'passionately [1] kind and angry'.

Jonson wrote different types of play from Shakespeare and Marlowe. *Volpone* is about a man who loves money and *The Alchemist* is about a man who isn't **honest**.

There were many other dramatists and poets in Britain at this time. It was a 'golden age' of English literature.

1. **passionately**：激烈地

The text and **beyond**

1 Comprehension check

Complete this fact file about Marlowe and Shakespeare. Write a number or word(s) in each gap.

	Marlowe	Shakespeare
Dates, birthplace	(1) ....-......... (2)	1564-1616 Stratford-upon- (6) ....
Other activities	Spy	Looking after (7) .... outside the theatre
He wrote*:	(3)	(8) ....
He married:	—	Anne Hathaway
Other information	Perhaps he was a member of 'The School of (4) ....'	His plays were performed at The Globe and (9) ....
Unusual fact	Some people think that he wrote (5)...................'s plays.	His friends (10) .... his plays after he died.

* give the name of one play mentioned in the chapter

2 Living dangerously

Read the section 'Living dangerously' again. Are sentences 1-5 'Right' (A) or 'Wrong' (B)? If there is not enough information to answer A or B, choose 'Doesn't Say' (C). Write A, B or C in the space. There is an example (0).

0	Marlowe stopped studying at Cambridge in 1587.	..A..
1	Many people know *Doctor Faustus*.	....
2	In the play, Faustus is sorry for his actions.	....
3	Marlowe went to prison for a long time.	....
4	'The School of Night' is the name of a play by Marlowe.	....
5	Thomas Kyd did not like Marlowe.	....

KET ③ An evening at the theatre

Complete this email. Write ONE word for each space 1-8. There is an example (0).

Hi Kate,

How (0) ..are........ you? I saw (1) .... play by Shakespeare at the Globe Theatre (2) .... London last night. It was *Othello*. The play is about a man (3) .... kills his wife (4) .... he thinks she loves another man. We had (5) .... stand all the time, like the people who watched Shakespeare's plays (6) .... the sixteenth century. We (7) .... very tired!

(8) .... you like to come with me to see another play at the Globe?

Love,

Dan

Before you read

① Vocabulary

Write the words in bold next to the correct definition 1-5. Use a dictionary to help you.

In the eighteenth century, **society** was very important. Some writers had good friends but they also had bad **enemies**! People called it the Age of **Reason** or the **Enlightenment**. Many writers wanted to be **witty**.

1	people who don't like you	....
2	the group of people around you	....
3	funny, in a clever way	....
4	using your mind, using your intelligence	....
5	period of history when people believed in the 'light' of knowledge	....

② You will read about two writers who had problems with their health. Milton was <u>blind</u>. Pope's enemies called him a '<u>hunchbacked toad</u>'. Use a dictionary to help you find out what the underlined words mean.

CHAPTER TWO

Seventeenth- and Eighteenth- Century Writers

思考人性

John Milton
Alexander Pope

A blind poet

John Milton was probably the most important British poet of the seventeenth century. Near the end of his life, in 1667, he wrote his greatest work. *Paradise Lost*, a poem with more than 10,000 lines, tells the story of Adam and Eve. But at this time in his life Milton was **blind**, so he 'wrote' the poem in his head and then his assistants wrote it on paper.

Perhaps the most interesting character in the poem is Satan [1]. He is interesting because Milton tells us how he feels and thinks. Like Dante's *Divina Commedia*, Milton's *Paradise Lost* is an important work in Western literature.

Milton's early life

John Milton was born in London on 9 December 1608. He studied at Cambridge University but he didn't enjoy it and had to leave

---

1. **Satan** : 撒旦

after one year because he disagreed with his teacher. However, he returned later and wrote his first poems.

After Cambridge, Milton studied at home and wrote more poetry. He had a good friend, Edward King, who died in 1637. Milton wrote one of his most beautiful poems, *Lycidas*, about Edward's death. Milton was a very clever man: he knew Latin, Greek, Hebrew [1], French, Spanish, Italian, Dutch and old English. In 1638 he travelled through Europe.

War and execution [2]

In the seventeenth century Protestants and Roman Catholics were often against each other in England. When Charles I became king in 1625, he wanted the King to be more important than the Government. Some people thought that Charles agreed with the Catholics but the Government wanted a Protestant England. In 1642 a civil war [3] began between the Royalists and the Government. The English Civil War, as it is called, changed Milton's life. He was for the Government and against the King. He wrote political and religious books, not only poetry. He wrote about freedom of the newspapers, about law and education and divorce [4]. People didn't like his ideas about marriage and called him 'Milton the Divorcer'. In 1642, he married Mary Powell. He was 33 and she was 16 years old. They were unhappy together and Mary left Milton to live back with her family, who agreed with the King. Perhaps that was why he was

1. **Hebrew** : 希伯來文
2. **execution** : 行刑
3. **a civil war** : 內戰
4. **divorce** : 離婚

interested in divorce. But in 1645, Mary returned. They had two daughters, Anne and Mary.

The Government won the Civil War and in 1649 King Charles I was executed. Probably Milton saw the execution. Other countries in Europe thought that the killing of the King was wrong, but Milton didn't and he wrote that England was right to remove the King. Now, Oliver Cromwell was 'Lord Protector' and England became for a short period a republic[1].

1652 was an unhappy year for Milton. Firstly, he became blind. Then his wife, Mary, died. Before her death, Mary had another daughter but, later the same year, Milton's only son died. He was one year old. Milton got married again in 1656 and had another daughter. But his new wife and daughter died the next year.

The return of the King

Oliver Cromwell died in 1658 and in 1660 King Charles I's son returned to England. He was also called Charles. Milton hid but after Charles II became King, they burnt Milton's republican writings, arrested him and put him in prison for a few months.

However, Milton got married again and continued to work on *Paradise Lost*. When he finally published this poem in 1667,

The Fall of the Rebel Angels,
engraving[2] (about 1868)
by Gustave Doré.

1. **a republic** : 共和國
2. **engraving** : 版畫

other writers understood that Milton was an important poet. In November 1674, Milton died. You can see his memorial [1] in Poets' Corner in Westminster Abbey.

The Age of Reason

The eighteenth century was the time of the **Enlightenment**. It is also often called the Age of **Reason**. People were interested in **society**. Because many thought that reason was very important in Classical times, new buildings were in the style of the Greeks and Romans, as you can see in cities like Bath. This was the neo-Classical age.

Alexander Pope is the most famous neo-Classical poet. His poetry is clever and **witty** [2]. He wrote many famous lines such as 'to err is human; to forgive divine.' [3]

The Royal Crescent in Bath (1767-75).

1. **a memorial** : 紀念雕像
2. **witty** : 風趣
3. **'to err is human; to forgive divine'**: 人皆有錯，寬恕乃大。

The Hunchbacked Toad

Like Milton, Pope had problems because of the religious situation in Britain. Pope came from a Catholic family and so he couldn't go to university or work for the government. He was born in 1688, in London, but his family moved out to a village near Windsor in 1700 because of a new law against Catholics. Catholic schools were illegal but Pope went to secret Catholic schools or studied at home.

When Pope was a child, he became ill with tuberculosis [1], a terrible illness that killed many people. As a result, he had asthma [2], a breathing illness, and headaches. Also, his body didn't develop normally so even when he was an adult he was only 1.37 metres tall. He had to wear a special piece of clothing for his back and one of his **enemies** called him a '**hunchbacked toad**' [3].

A poem about a piece of hair

Pope spent a lot of time in his father's library when he was young. He said that he wrote his first poem when he was 12. When he was 23, he published *The Essay on Criticism*.

At about this time, Pope wrote a comic poem called *The Rape of the Lock*: here, 'rape' means to take without telling the owner and a 'lock' is a small piece of hair. It is about a man who cuts some hair from a girl's head and then she becomes angry. This really happened and Pope's long poem about it is very funny.

1. **tuberculosis**：肺結核
2. **asthma**：哮喘
3. **a hunchbacked toad**：駝背的討厭鬼

Alexander Pope's Villa in Twickenham (about 1759) by Samuel Scott.

Friends and enemies

Pope wasn't an easy person to know. He often disagreed with other writers and wrote about them in a bad way. In 1712, Pope and some other writers called themselves the 'Scriblerus Club'. The writers of this club wrote poetry to attack other writers. Of course, they made many enemies by doing this.

Pope loved Homer and Shakespeare. He translated Homer's long poems with the help of other writers. They became angry when Pope didn't publish their names in the book. He also published Shakespeare's plays after changing them by writing some parts in a more 'neo-classical' way. Some people said that it was a bad thing to do. He answered them by writing *The Dunciad*, a poem that called his enemies stupid. The title comes from the English word for a stupid person, a 'dunce'.

After he became famous, Pope moved to a house in Twickenham, near London. Many people visited Pope and enjoyed his beautiful gardens and a famous grotto [1].

Pope died in 1744. After some years, a new generation of poets was approaching. They were the Romantics.

---

1. **a grotto** : 石窟

The text and **beyond**

1 **Comprehension check**

Complete this fact file about John Milton and Alexander Pope. Write a number or word(s) in each gap.

	John Milton	Alexander Pope
Dates	**(1)** ....-............	**(8)** ....-............
Disabilities	In **(2)** .... , he became blind.	only **(9)** .... tall as an adult.
Period	He wrote in the **(3)** .... century.	He wrote in the **(10)** .... of ....
Poems	*Lycidas* — for his friend, Edward **(4)** .... *Paradise Lost*	*The Rape of the* **(11)** .... *The Essay on Criticism* *The Dunciad*
Important events	1625: **(5)** .... became 1642 King: a **(6)** .... started in 1660 England: **(7)** .... became King	1700: a new anti-Catholic **(12)** ....

2 *Paradise Lost*

Read the sections 'A blind poet' and 'The return of the King' again. Fill in the information on the form. There is an example (0).

> **Book Record**
>
> **Title: (0)** Paradise Lost ....
> **Author: (1)** ....
> **Date of Publication: (2)** ....
> **Length: (3)** .... lines
> **Main characters:** Adam, Eve and **(4)** ....
> **Similar European works: (5)** ....

2 ACTIVITIES

Read the section 'Friends and enemies' again. Are sentences 1-5 'Right' (A) or 'Wrong' (B)? If there is not enough information to answer A or B, choose 'Doesn't Say' (C). Write A, B or C in the space.

1   The Scriblerus Club was a meeting place for writers.   ....
2   Pope translated Homer's poems without help from
    other writers.   ....
3   Pope wrote *The Dunciad* in 1712.   ....
4   Pope's house and gardens in Twickenham were beautiful.   ....
5   Pope was one of the Romantics.   ....

Before you read

① Vocabulary

In Chapter Three, you will read about different types of people. Match sentences 1-3 with the words A-C. Use a dictionary if necessary.

A philosopher   B vampire   C genius

1   ☐   this person is very clever and does great things
2   ☐   this person thinks about ideas and the meaning of life
3   ☐   this person drinks the blood of other people!

② Write sentences 1-4 again. Use words from the box instead of the underlined words.

> buried (past form of *to bury*)   an empire   freedom   love affairs

1   Napoleon wanted to have ***a lot of countries which belonged to his country.***
2   But the people in these countries wanted ***to be free***.
3   Napoleon had many ***relationships with women.***
4   In Paris, you can visit the place where they ***put the dead body of*** Napoleon.

CHAPTER THREE

The Romantics

浪漫詩人

George Gordon, Lord Byron
Percy Bysshe Shelley
William Wordsworth
Samuel Taylor Coleridge
John Keats

After the Age of Reason, writers, musicians and artists became interested in the imagination. They thought that nature — for example mountains, lakes and the sea — was more important than human society. They loved **freedom**. Many of them believed in the idea of individual **genius**. This was the time of Romanticism.

At the end of the eighteenth and beginning of the nineteenth century in Britain, five Romantic poets became famous — Wordsworth and Coleridge, Byron, Shelley and Keats. They wrote poetry which was different from that of the poets who lived before them.

'Mad, bad and dangerous to know'

Lord Byron lived from 1788 to 1824. He was very good-looking but he was born with a bad foot, so he walked badly all his life. His name was George Gordon but when he was ten years old a great-uncle died and he became 'Lord Byron'.

Lady Caroline Lamb was one of the women who loved Lord

Byron. She said that he was 'mad, bad and dangerous to know.' Many people in Britain were interested in him because he was unusual. When he was at Cambridge University, he wanted to have a dog. This was against the university rules, so he had a bear in his rooms!

Byron loved travelling. In 1809, after he finished university, he visited a lot of European countries. It was a dangerous time in Europe: Napoleon's soldiers were everywhere. Byron travelled around the Mediterranean and even went to Albania. When he returned to England, he published his poems and lots of readers quickly bought them. Byron said that he woke up one morning and discovered that he was famous.

It isn't easy to be famous. Everyone talked about his love life. Lady Caroline loved him but Byron began to see other women. Lady Caroline couldn't forget him and became thin and ill. Byron married her cousin but the marriage was unhappy and soon finished. Some people even said that he was in love with his half-sister[1], Augusta.

One poet, two wives

Percy Bysshe Shelley was younger than Byron. He was born in 1792. He went to Eton school, the most famous in England, but he didn't enjoy it. The other boys pulled his clothes and stole his books. He didn't like Oxford University either. He knew that he

1. **a half-sister** : 同父異母的姐妹

was a special person, different from the other students. Shelley had to leave university in 1811 because he wrote that there was no God in a short book called *The Necessity of Atheism* [1].

When Shelley was 19, he married Harriet Westbrook. But the young poet wasn't a good husband. In 1814, Shelley met Mary Godwin and fell in love with her. Mary was the daughter of a **philosopher**, William Godwin, and a famous feminist, Mary Wollstonecraft. Shelley left Harriet and their child. He ran away with Mary to Switzerland. Later, poor Harriet killed herself in the Serpentine lake in London in 1816. A few weeks after this, Shelley married Mary.

Byron and Shelley

What happened when Shelley met Byron? These two young men loved poetry, love and freedom. They both disagreed with British society and they didn't like the political system in Europe.

In summer 1816, Shelley, Mary and Byron lived together near Lake Geneva in Switzerland. The Romantic poets were excited by the lakes and mountains of the Alps. But the weather that summer was cold and stormy. One wet night, the poets and Mary

1. **atheism** : 無神論

The Funeral of Shelley (1889) by Louis Edouard Fournier.

had a competition. Who could write the best ghost story? Byron wrote about a **vampire**. The story was finished by his friend and doctor John Polidori, and became the first vampire story in English. But Mary Shelley wrote the best story, about a science student who made a new human being. She was only nineteen years old. Later she published the book and now it is very famous — *Frankenstein*.

Both Byron and Shelley wanted to leave England. There was a lot of talk about them in the newspapers and magazines. They loved Italy and stayed in several Italian cities. They wrote some of their most famous poems there.

'A beautiful and ineffectual angel' [1]

On 8 July, 1822, Shelley went sailing with a friend in the Golfo di Spezia in north-west Italy. There was a great storm and the boat went down. Shelley died in the sea. He was only twenty-nine years old.

A week later, the sea carried Shelley's body to the beach. His friends decided to burn his body there. Byron didn't want

1. '**a beautiful and ineffectual angel** ': 美麗而柔弱的天使

26

to watch and swam out to sea, but Trelawney, another writer, stayed. As the fire burnt, Trelawney put his hand into the fire and pulled out Shelley's heart.

Byron and Greece

In Italy, Byron had a **love affair** with Teresa, Contessa Guiccioli and she left her husband for Byron. Like all his love affairs, this one was very short.

However, Byron's greatest love affair was with freedom. At the beginning of 19th century there were two great **empires** in Europe, the Austrian Empire and the Turkish Empire. Byron wanted to help small nations become independent from these empires.

In 1823, Byron decided to help the Greeks, who were controlled by the Turkish Empire. Together with a Greek leader, he wanted to fight the Turkish army at Lepanto. But in February he became ill. On 19 April 1824, Lord Byron died. He was 36 years old.

The Greeks loved Lord Byron. After he died, they **buried** his heart at Missolonghi. Even now, Byron is more famous in other European countries than in Britain. His most famous poems are 'She Walks in Beauty', *Childe Harold* and *Don Juan*.

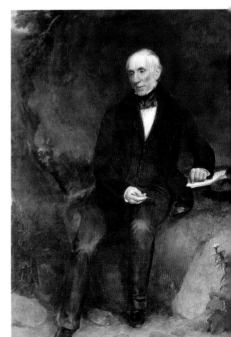

The first 'Romantic poets'

Byron and Shelley weren't the first Romantic poets in England. In 1798, William Wordworth and Samuel Taylor Coleridge published their poems together in a book called *Lyrical Ballads*. They wrote in simple language about people and nature.

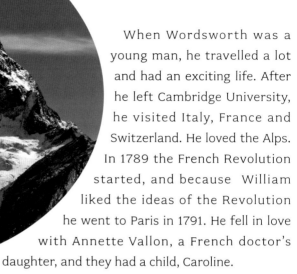

When Wordsworth was a young man, he travelled a lot and had an exciting life. After he left Cambridge University, he visited Italy, France and Switzerland. He loved the Alps. In 1789 the French Revolution started, and because William liked the ideas of the Revolution he went to Paris in 1791. He fell in love with Annette Vallon, a French doctor's daughter, and they had a child, Caroline.

Wordsworth returned to England and he didn't see Annette or his daughter Caroline again for many years because there was a war between England and France. Finally, he decided not to marry Annette.

Books, love, spies and drugs

Samuel Taylor Coleridge was Wordsworth's friend. Coleridge was a very clever man; when he was a child, he spent a lot of time in the library reading books. His family sent him to a school in London and he was often alone. Books were his friends.

When he was a young man he decided to go to America with some friends and begin a new, perfect society. He married Sarah Fricker. He didn't really love her but he married her because one of these friends married her sister. His friends changed their minds and Coleridge never went to America. But he had a wife!

When Coleridge met Wordsworth and his sister, Dorothy, they quickly became friends. They lived near each other in Somerset in south-west England and enjoyed the beautiful countryside. The three friends often walked in the countryside at night with pens and paper. They were writing poems. When people saw this, they thought that they were French spies and told the government in London.

However, Coleridge had a problem. At this time, doctors often gave opium [1] as a medicine. When Coleridge had toothache or an illness, he took opium, but then he couldn't live without it. Many people think that he wrote the poem 'Kubla Khan' under the effect of the opium.

The Lake Poets

Because they loved nature, Wordsworth and Coleridge went to live in the Lake District. This is a beautiful area of lakes and hills in the north-west of England. Wordsworth was born there in 1770 and, after 1800, lived there for the rest of his life. Another poet, Robert Southey, went there too and people called them 'the Lake Poets'.

In 1799, the two poets stayed at a farm in Yorkshire and fell in love with two sisters. William married Mary Hutchinson but Coleridge couldn't marry Sara Hutchinson. He was very unhappy.

1. **opium** : 鴉片

View of Lake Grasmere,
Cumbria, England.

Wordsworth moved to Dove Cottage in the Lake District and lived with his wife and his sister, Dorothy.

Coleridge's health became worse because he continued taking opium. He quarrelled with Wordsworth and moved away from the Lakes. He published a magazine about books and philosophy and gave a famous talk on *Hamlet* by Shakespeare. Finally, he was so ill that he went to live with a doctor in London. He died in 1834.

Coleridge's most famous poem is *The Rime of the Ancient Mariner*. The poem tells the story of a sailor who kills an albatross, a large seabird. This brings the ship bad luck and the other sailors put the dead bird round the sailor's neck. Everyone on the ship dies except the 'ancient mariner'. After terrible adventures, he understands that it was wrong to kill the bird and returns to England. This was perhaps the first 'green', environmental poem — if you don't look after nature, you will have a bad life.

William Wordsworth lived until he was 80. If you visit the London Eye in London, you can see one of his poems there, 'Upon Westminster Bridge'. The poem is about London when the city is quiet in the early morning.

The Mariner Shoots the Albatross, engraving (1877) by Gustave Doré.

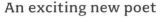

An exciting new poet

When Shelley died in the sea, he had a book of poems by John Keats in his jacket. In 1817, a young poet met William Wordsworth at a dinner party. This was John Keats. He read one of his poems to Wordsworth, who didn't enjoy it very much.

Keats was different. He didn't go to Oxford or Cambridge University. He wasn't from a rich family. But he loved poetry. Keats was the oldest son and after his father died, he felt that he had to look after his family — his mother, his brothers Tom and George and his young sister, Fanny.

Keats studied medicine. One of his friends said that when Keats was in a class he wrote poetry instead of listening to the teacher. When he published his first poem in a magazine, other writers liked it and helped him. He decided to stop studying medicine and become a poet. His first book of poems was published in 1816.

Two Men Contemplating the Moon (about 1819-20) by Caspar David Friedrich.

Eilean Donan Castle in north-east Scotland.

Love and death

Keats's mother died from tuberculosis, and at the end of 1817 Keats's younger brother Tom had the same illness. His other brother, George, decided to live in America. But Keats wasn't alone. He had many good friends. He travelled through Britain with one of these friends, Charles Brown. They visited the Lake District and Scotland but Keats returned when he himself was ill.

Back in London, Keats stayed with Charles Brown and met the Brawne family, his neighbours. Fanny Brawne was eighteen years old and very pretty. Tom, his brother, was now very ill. On 1 December 1818, Tom died and Keats was very sad.

The final journey

1819 was a wonderful year for Keats. He wrote some of his greatest poems and Fanny Brawne fell in love with him. During this year, they wanted to get married but he was poor and couldn't marry her. He wrote a poem to her, 'Bright Star'; a lot of his poems are about life and death. He was only 23 years old but his poems were beautiful.

But 1820 was a terrible year. On 3 February, Keats was out in the bad weather. He came back to Brown's house with a high temperature and went to bed. Keats had tuberculosis.

Charles Brown looked after Keats and when Brown went away for the summer, Keats stayed with the Brawne family and Fanny was his nurse. The doctors were worried: England was very cold and wet, so they decided to send him to Italy to get better.

Keats went to Rome with another friend, a young painter, Joseph Severn. Fanny and Keats said goodbye — she gave him presents and wrote to him often when he was in Italy. But Keats didn't open her letters. He knew he was dying and he was sad when he thought about their love.

Keats's house (left) in Piazza di Spagna, Rome.

At first, Keats could walk around the city and loved the Italian way of life. But his illness got worse. He asked Severn to **bury** a piece of Fanny Brawne's hair and a purse from his sister, Fanny, with him. On 26 February 1821, Keats died.

He was buried in the Protestant cemetery [1] in Rome. After Keats's death, Shelley wrote a long poem, *Adonais*, about Keats and two years later, Shelley's heart was buried in the same cemetery.

'Writ in water'

Fanny Brawne was sad after Keats died. She read his love letters to her again and again. Later, she married, but she never forgot the young poet who was in love with her.

Keats asked for these words to be on his gravestone [2]:

'Here lies one whose name was writ [3] in water.'

This means that nobody will remember his name. He thought this because some writers in magazines and newspapers wrote unkind things about his poems. Of course, he was wrong. He also said:

'I think I shall be among the English Poets after my death.'

This is true.

All the Romantic poets are now famous, nearly two hundred years later. They changed the way that we think about poetry, about nature and about love.

1. **a cemetery** : 墳場
2. **gravestone** : 墓碑
3. **writ** : 寫在

The text and **beyond**

1 **Comprehension check**

Complete this fact file about Byron and Shelley. Write a number or word(s) in each gap.

	Byron	Shelley
Dates	(1) ....-............	(8) ....-............
Marriage	He was married to Lady Caroline's (2)	He was married to Harriet (9) ....
Other relationships	Augusta, his half- (3) .... Lady (4) .... Contessa (5)	After Harriet killed herself, he married (10) .... , who wrote (11) ....
Unusual facts	He had a (6) .... when he was at university.	He had to leave university because he wrote against religion.
Deaths	He went to (7) .... to fight against the Turkish Empire but died there.	He (12) .... in the Golfo di Spezia.

2 **The first 'Romantic poets'**

Read the section 'The first Romantic poets' again. Are sentences 1-5 'Right' (A) or 'Wrong' (B)? If there is not enough information to answer A or B, choose 'Doesn't Say' (C). Write A, B or C in the space.

1 Byron and Shelley knew Wordsworth well.   ....
2 In 1798, poems by two Romantic poets were published.   ....
3 Wordsworth's daughter was called Caroline.   ....
4 Wordsworth sometimes saw Annette during the war.   ....
5 Annette was angry when Wordsworth didn't marry her. ....

3 ACTIVITIES

3 Questions in the past

Look at the section 'Books, love, spies and drugs' again. Then complete these questions about Wordsworth and Coleridge. Write one word in each space. There is an example (0).

0 What ...did... Coleridge ...do.... when he was a child?
   He spent a lot of time reading books.

1 .... his family .... him to a school in Scotland?
   No, to a school in London.

2 Where .... Coleridge .... to go?
   To America.

3 .... Coleridge .... to America?
   No, he didn't.

4 .... Coleridge, Wordsworth and his sister ....?
   In Somerset.

5 .... the people ....?
   They reported them to the government.

KET **4** Daffodils

Read about Wordsworth's daffodils. Choose the best word (A, B or C) for each space 1-6. There is an example (0).

Daffodils

Wordsworth's (0) .... famous poem is probably 'I wandered lonely as a cloud', a poem about daffodils in the Lake District. You can see yellow daffodils (1) ..A. the spring in most English gardens. But Wordsworth wrote about daffodils in the countryside. Many people thought that the language of (2) .... poem was too simple. But later it (3) .... very popular. Perhaps Wordsworth used the ideas of (4) .... sister Dorothy. She also (5) .... about these flowers in her diary. (6) .... 15 June 1802, she wrote, 'We saw a few daffodils close to the water.'

0	(A) most	**B** more	**C** much
1	**A** on	**B** at	**C** in
2	**A** a	**B** the	**C** one
3	**A** become	**B** becomes	**C** became
4	**A** their	**B** his	**C** her
5	**A** said	**B** told	**C** wrote
6	**A** In	**B** On	**C** At

 5 Writing

Your friend's girlfriend likes poetry. He wants to give her a present. Write an email to him. Tell him:

- the **name** of one Romantic poet
- **something about** this writer
- **where** to buy a book by this writer for his girlfriend

Write 25-35 words.

INTERNET PROJECT

The Poetry of the Romantics

Connect to the internet and go to www.blackcat-cideb.com or www.cideb.it. Insert the title or part of the title of this book into our search engine. Open the page for *Great British Writers*. Click on the Internet project link. Go down the page until you find the title of this book and click on the link for this project.

Find out which Romantic poets wrote these lines. Which poems do they come from? Use a dictionary for any words which you don't understand.

1 She walks in beauty like the night…
2 I saw a crowd, a host of golden daffodils…
3 Look on my works, ye mighty, and despair!
4 Beauty is truth, truth beauty
5 Water, water, everywhere, Nor any drop to drink.
6 Thoughts that… lie too deep for tears.

Writers and Places

作家故居

Many places in Britain are connected with writers. Stratford-upon-Avon is famous because of Shakespeare. Dickens is connected with London and Rochester and Thomas Hardy is connected with Wessex. Here are three other places.

Keats's House in Hampstead, London.

Keats's House

Keats's House is in Hampstead, in north-west London. John Keats lived here from 1818 to 1820. He wrote his most famous poems while he lived there, such as 'Ode to a Grecian Urn', and he fell in love with the girl who lived next door, Fanny Brawne. You can visit the house and see manuscripts [1], letters, paintings and so on connected with Keats and other Romantic poets. You can also see the ring that he gave to Fanny and a piece of her hair. His friend, Charles Brown, said that Keats wrote his poem 'Ode to a Nightingale [2]' when he was sitting under a tree in the garden.

In Rome, on the Spanish steps in the Piazza di Spagna, you can visit the house where Keats stayed with his friend Joseph Severn.

1. **manuscripts** : 手稿
2. **a nightingale** : 夜鶯

William Wordsworth's manuscripts and books at Dove Cottage.

Dove Cottage

William Wordsworth and his sister Dorothy lived at Dove Cottage from 1799 to 1808. It is in the village of Grasmere in the Lake District. In 1802, William's wife, Mary Hutchinson, went to live there too. William wrote many famous poems while he lived here. From the windows, he could see Grasmere lake and the beautiful valley.

You can also see his birthplace, now called Wordsworth House, in Cockermouth on the coast. Rydal House is also open to visitors; this is the house where Wordsworth lived at the end of his life. Rydal House has wonderful views of the lakes and the hills.

Haworth

The Brontë sisters (you will meet them in the next chapter) wrote many of their novels in their father's house in the village of Haworth. The village is on a hill in Yorkshire, in the north-east of England. Now you can visit the house and see a lot of the furniture, books and decoration, which are the same as when the sisters lived there.

You can go there by car or by bus from the city of Bradford. On some days in the summer you can travel to Haworth by steam train [1] . *Wuthering Heights* is popular with many nationalities.

The countryside around Haworth is beautiful and wild. It is very important in the books of the sisters, especially in *Wuthering Heights*. Nowadays, this area is usually called 'Brontë Country'.

1 Comprehension check

Now answer the following questions.

Which writer/s...

1   could see lakes from his house?
2   was born near the sea?
3   wrote about a place called Wessex?
4   was Fanny Brawne's neighbour?

1.   **a steam train** :

INTERNET PROJECT

Stratford-upon-Avon and Shakespeare

Connect to the internet and go to www.blackcat-cideb.com or www.cideb.it. Insert the title of the book into our search engine. Open the page for *Great British Writers*. Click on the Internet project link. Go down the page until you find the title of this book and click on the relevant link for this project.

Look at the website about Stratford-upon-Avon and find the answers to the following questions.

1 What buildings can you visit in Stratford which are connected with the life of William Shakespeare?

2 Which company performs in the main theatre in Stratford?

3 In which church is Shakespeare buried?

4 In which house did Shakespeare's mother live when she was a child?

Before you read

1 Vocabulary

Match the words (a-e) to the descriptions (1-5).

> **a** middle classes   **b** honeymoon   **c** pregnant
> **d** ghost   **e** clergyman

1 ☐ We are the people from the middle of society.

2 ☐ I am a dead person who comes back to visit people who are still living.

3 ☐ I work for the Anglican church.

4 ☐ I am going to have a baby.

5 ☐ After they get married, the man and woman go on this special holiday.

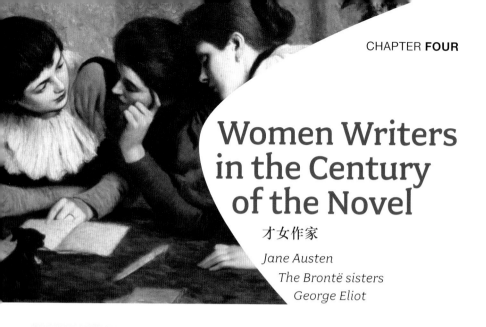

CHAPTER FOUR

Women Writers in the Century of the Novel

才女作家

Jane Austen
The Brontë sisters
George Eliot

Hidden identities

During the nineteenth century, novels became the most popular form of literature. People from the **middle classes** had time to read and enjoyed the realism [1] of novels. Many of the best writers were women. However, some men didn't think that women writers were good. As a result, some women novelists didn't use their true identity. Jane Austen published her novels without her name on them. The Brontë sisters used men's names when they first wrote. Mary Anne Evans wrote using the name of George Eliot.

Love and marriage

Jane Austen was born in 1775. During her life, she wrote six important novels — *Northanger Abbey, Sense and Sensibility, Pride and Prejudice, Mansfield Park, Emma* and *Persuasion*.

She didn't have an exciting life. However, she watched the

1. **realism**：現實主義

people around her carefully and used what she saw to create the characters in her novels.

Her novels end in marriage, but they are not simple love stories. They show that life was difficult for women in early nineteenth-century Britain, when men were more important in society. In *Pride and Prejudice*, Elizabeth Bennet marries Mr Darcy for love after many problems. But her friend marries a stupid husband because she wants to have a comfortable life.

Jane Austen herself didn't get married. We don't know a lot about her romantic life but we think that she fell in love with Tom Lefoy, a young man who wanted to study law in London. Jane wrote about him in letters to her sister, Cassandra, and perhaps they wanted to get married. But Tom's family wanted to find a rich wife for him. They sent him away and Jane and Tom never met again.

There is another story about Jane Austen and love. In 1801, Jane was on holiday at Sidmouth in Devon in the south west of England. She met a young **clergyman** and some people say that they fell in love. They wanted to meet again but before they did, the young man died.

In 1802, Harris Bigg Wither, the brother of a friend, asked Jane to marry him. Harris wasn't a very good-looking man but he came from a rich family and Jane knew that she could help her family. She said 'yes'. But next morning, she decided that she didn't want to marry him. This was the last person to ask Jane to marry him.

Becoming a writer

Jane Austen had six brothers and one sister, Cassandra. Three brothers were in the navy [1] and probably Jane used their experience [2] to write about officers in the navy, such as in *Persuasion*.

Jane grew up in Steventon, a village in the south of England. She was a girl but she had a lot of freedom. She read the books in her father's large library and when she was still a child she began to write stories. She wrote a novel called *Love and Freindship*. (look at Jane's spelling mistake!) and *The History of England*. Cassandra Austen painted pictures for Jane's books.

In 1793, when she was eighteen, Jane decided to become a professional writer. Women writers such as Fanny Burney and Maria Edgeworth were already popular but Jane wrote her own kind of novel. However people didn't think that women writers could write good books, so it was difficult for them to be successful.

Anne Elliot with her cousin, William Elliot, from *Persuasion* by Jane Austen, engraving (about 1894) by Hugh Thomson.

Money problems

In 1800, the family moved to Bath, a very fashionable city in the eighteenth and early nineteenth centuries. Perhaps Jane didn't like living in Bath because it was so different from the village of Steventon. When her father died, in 1805, the family didn't have much money.

1. **navy** : 海軍
2. **experience** : 經歷

Scene from the BBC TV film *Persuasion* (1995) directed by Roger Michell.

In 1809, Jane, her mother and Cassandra moved to Chawton in Hampshire, in the south of England. In this house Jane Austen wrote her greatest novels. People say that the door to her room made a noise but that Jane didn't want anyone to repair it. When she heard the noise, she knew that someone was coming so that she could hide her writing.

Her books were popular and she earned some money from them. The Prince Regent enjoyed her books and Jane was asked to put the Prince's name in her next novel. Jane didn't like the Prince but she put his name in the front of *Emma*.

In 1816, Jane became very ill. She found it difficult to walk or do any work but she continued to write. In 1817, she travelled to Winchester to see a doctor but while she was there, she died. She is buried in Winchester Cathedral. After she died, Cassandra and Henry Austen published two of her novels, *Persuasion* and *Northanger Abbey*, for the first time. Henry wrote that his sister, Jane Austen, was the writer. This was the first time that her name was written in her books.

Three sisters

Jane Austen wrote about feelings in a clever, ironic [1] way but later in the nineteenth century, during the late Romantic period, three sisters wrote exciting novels about love. Their names were Charlotte, Emily and Anne Brontë.

In the north of England there is a wild area of high, open land. This type of land is called a 'moor'. Few people live there and the weather is often stormy. In this area, in the village of Haworth, the family of Patrick Brontë and his wife lived from 1821.

The Brontë Sisters (about 1834) by their brother, Patrick Branwell Brontë. From the left: Anne, Emily and Charlotte.

They weren't a lucky family. Maria, the mother, died after they moved to Haworth. Charlotte and Emily were sent away from home to the Clergy Daughters School in Lancashire with two other sisters, Maria and Elizabeth. The conditions at the school were very bad and Maria and Elizabeth died because of this.

Angria and Gondal

The three sisters, with their brother, Branwell, all wrote long stories when they were children. Branwell had some toy soldiers and the first stories were about the lives of these soldiers. They imagined countries and wrote about their histories. Charlotte wrote with Branwell about a place called 'Angria' while Emily and Anne wrote about 'Gondal'. The stories were very complicated [2] and prepared them well for their lives as writers.

1. **ironic** : 諷刺
2. **complicated** : 複雜

Charlotte

Charlotte was born in 1816. From 1839 to 1841, she worked as a governess, looking after and teaching the children of other families. In 1842, with Emily, she went to live with the family of Constantin and Claire Heger, in Brussels. Charlotte taught English and Emily taught music. Charlotte fell in love with Constantin Heger. This love for a married man made her very unhappy but later she wrote two novels using her experience.

Back in Haworth, the three sisters published poetry and novels under men's names: Charlotte called herself Currer Bell, Emily was Ellis Bell and Anne was Acton Bell.

Charlotte's most famous novel is *Jane Eyre*. The story is about a girl who has a terrible time as a child. She goes to a school where the conditions are very bad and Jane's best friend dies. Later in the novel, Jane becomes a governess and wants to marry the man who she works for, Mr Rochester. But Rochester is

Scene from the film *Jane Eyre* (1996) directed by Franco Zeffirelli.

Scene from the film *Wuthering Heights* (1992) directed by Peter Kosminsky.

already married to a mad wife who lives in secret in his house. You can see that Jane Eyre's life is like some parts of Charlotte's life. But finally, Jane marries Mr Rochester.

When Charlotte gave her father *Jane Eyre*, he told the family, 'Children, Charlotte has written a book and it is a better one than I expected.'

Charlotte Brontë liked writing about strong, independent women. She didn't like the novels of Jane Austen because she thought that the women characters weren't independent.

Emily and Anne

Emily was born in 1818. Like Charlotte, she worked as a governess. Emily wrote only one novel but it became very famous.

Wuthering Heights tells the story of the love between Catherine (Cathy) Earnshaw and Heathcliff. Their love story is as wild and exciting as the **moor**, where it takes place. When Cathy dies, Heathcliff becomes a terrible person. However, he never forgets Cathy and speaks to her **ghost** as he walks on the moor.

This story of a strong love that lasts even after death interests readers today just as it did when Emily wrote it.

Anne Brontë is less famous than her sisters. However, she also wrote novels. The best known is *The Tenant of Wildfell Hall*. Like her sisters, she worked for a period as a governess. She tried to help her brother, Branwell, by getting him a job as a private teacher with the Robinson family. But Branwell lost the job after he had a love affair with Mrs Robinson.

Unhappy endings

Branwell had an unhappy adult life. He drank too much and took opium. He died in 1848. The weather at his funeral [1] was cold and Emily became ill because of it. She then died in December 1848. Anne Brontë died in May 1849. Branwell was thirty-one years old, Emily was thirty and Anne was twenty-eight when they died.

Charlotte lived longer. She visited London and met famous writers. However, she spent most of her time at Haworth because she wanted to look after her father. In 1854, she married and became **pregnant**. But before the child was born, Charlotte became ill and she and the baby died.

All three sisters had short lives. However, it is very unusual for so many people in one family to be important writers. The Brontë sisters wrote about a new kind of woman who was strong and unafraid. They changed the idea of women characters in novels.

1. **a funeral** : 葬禮

A writer with many names

Another writer changed the way that people thought about women writers. She wrote as 'George Eliot' but her real name was Mary Anne (or Mary Ann) Evans.

She was born in 1819, in Arbury, in the middle of England. Her father, Robert Evans, was the manager of the land for an important family. When she was a child, Mary Anne read many of the books in the library at Arbury Hall, the home of her father's employers, and she began to love literature.

When she was twenty-one, she moved with her father to a house near Coventry and met Charles and Cara Bray. She met some famous writers and philosophers. Before this, Mary Anne had a strong religious education but the people that she met now often had different ideas about religion and the truth of the Bible.

After her father died, she travelled to Switzerland with the Brays and lived alone in Geneva for a short period. In 1850, she returned to London to become a professional writer. She worked with John Chapman on a political magazine, *The Westminster Review*. People were surprised that a woman was doing an important job. It was the time of Queen Victoria and a woman was usually a wife, not an independent worker.

Mary Anne wasn't a beautiful woman. She had a large nose and a plain face. But people who met her said that she was a beautiful person. In 1851, she met George Henry Lewes and they fell in love. Lewes had a wife, Agnes, but it was an unusual marriage. Both Lewes and Agnes had other lovers and Agnes had children with other men. Lewes and Mary Anne decided to live together. They couldn't get married but she called herself Marian Evans Lewes.

Many people didn't like this. They said it was wrong for a man and a woman to live together if they weren't married. Lewes and Mary Anne lost most of their friends.

George Eliot is born

At this time, George Eliot was 'born'. Mary Anne decided to write and publish novels but she didn't want people to think that she was a 'silly' woman writer. Also, she knew that many people didn't like her now that she lived with Lewes. So, she used a different name to publish her books.

In 1859, 'George Eliot' published *Adam Bede*. It was a very successful novel. People wanted to know more about the writer. There was even a man, Joseph Liggins, who told people that he wrote it. Mary Anne decided to tell people that she was the true writer. Many people were surprised that a woman was able to write these good, clever books.

Her most famous novel is *Middlemarch*. The story doesn't take place in an exciting place like London or Paris but in a small town in the Midlands. One of the main characters is

Illustration (1885) by William Small for *Adam Bede* by George Eliot.

Dorothea Brooke, a clever woman who marries the wrong man and can't do the things that she wants to do. There are many other characters too, and Eliot describes their lives. The novel is not just a 'love story' but also includes politics, philosophy, religion and society.

A strange honeymoon

In 1878, Lewes died. Mary Anne met an American, John Walter Cross, who was twenty years younger than her. They got married in 1880. They went on **honeymoon** to Venice and a strange thing happened. Her new husband jumped out of the hotel room into the Grand Canal! He wasn't hurt but nobody knows why he did it.

The marriage was short. In December 1880, Mary Anne Evans died. She wanted to be buried in Westminster Abbey next to other great writers. But she wasn't a Christian, so it wasn't possible. However in 1980, a memorial was put in Poets' Corner in the Abbey. Henry James, the American writer, said that in her novels she created 'rich, deep, masterful pictures' of human life. She was the last of the great women novelists of the nineteenth century.

The Poets' Corner, Westminster Abbey, London.

The text and **beyond**

1 **Comprehension check**

Complete this fact file about Jane Austen and George Eliot. Write a number or word(s) in each gap.

	Jane Austen	George Eliot
Dates	**(1)** .... -	**(12)** .... - ....
Family & friends	six **(2)** .... and a sister called **(3)**	In Coventry, she met Charles and Cara **(13)** ....
She lived in:	Steventon **(4)** .... **(5)**	Arbury, Coventry and London. In London she edited a **(14)** ....
Love and marriage	Steventon: perhaps in love with **(6)** .... Sidmouth: a young clergyman who **(7)**	lived with: George Henry **(15)** .... married: **(16)** ....
Some of her novels	*Pride and* **(8)** ...., *Emma*	**(17)** ....
Unusual fact	She agreed to marry a man but said **(9)** .... the next day.	During their honeymoon, her husband jumped into the **(18)** ....in Venice.
Deaths	She died in **(10)** .... and is buried in the **(11)**	She was **(19)** .... buried in Westminster Abbey.

2 Write a similar fact file about Charlotte Brontë and Emily Brontë. Use the information in Chapter Four. Use these headings:

Dates   Love   Family   Early life   Famous novel   Unusual fact

4 ACTIVITIES

KET ③ The Brontë family

Read the sections 'Emily and Anne' and 'Unhappy endings' again. Are sentences 1-6 'Right' (A) or 'Wrong' (B)? If there is not enough information to answer A or B, choose 'Doesn't Say' (C). Write A, B or C in the space.

1   Emily wrote a lot of novels that weren't famous.   ....
2   Emily wrote about the countryside that she knew well.   ....
3   *The Tenant of Wildfell Hall* is a novel by Anne and her brother.   ....
4   Branwell had problems in his life.   ....
5   Emily did not wear warm clothes at Branwell's funeral.   ....
6   Branwell, Emily and Anne died before they were thirty.   ....

④ Vocabulary – opposites

Look at the underlined adjectives in these sentences from Chapter Four. What is the opposite of the adjective? There is an example (0).

0   She lived in <u>small</u> places for most of her life.   big OR large
1   They show that life was <u>difficult</u> for women.   ....
2   Her friend marries a <u>stupid</u> husband.   ....
3   Tom's family wanted to find a <u>rich</u> wife for him.   ....
4   They weren't a <u>lucky</u> family.   ....
5   Charlotte was the <u>oldest</u> daughter.   ....
6   This made her very <u>unhappy</u>.   ....
7   The conditions are very <u>bad</u>.   ....
8   Mary Anne wasn't a <u>beautiful</u> woman.   ....

KET ⑤ Writing

Your friend has to write about Emily Brontë for homework. Write a note to help him. Tell him:

• **when and where** she lived   • the **name** of her novel
• the **names** of her sisters

Write 25-35 words.

6 **Speaking: hobbies**

When the Brontë sisters were children, their hobby was writing. Talk about one of your hobbies with a partner. Also, ask your partner questions about his/her hobby.

Talk about:

1   when you began the hobby
2   where you do this activity
3   how often you do this activity (e.g. every week, every month)
4   how much you like this hobby

Before you read

1 **Vocabulary**

Match the words in the box with sentences 1-4.

generous   to owe   poverty   slavery

1   you enjoy giving things to other people = you are ....

2   being very poor = living in ....

3   selling and buying people = ...

4   you need to pay money to other people = ... money.

You are going to read about Thomas Hardy. *Fate* is an important idea in his novels. *Fate* means that there is a plan for our lives: we can't change the things that are going to happen to us. In Hardy's novels, *fate* is often *cruel*. This means that *fate* hurts us and our lives end sadly.

55

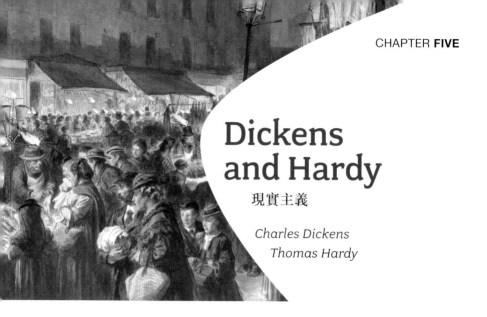

Dickens and Hardy

現實主義

Charles Dickens
Thomas Hardy

A child worker

In 1824, a 12-year-old boy worked in a factory in London. His father was in prison because he **owed** [1] money to people. The factory building was dark and in a bad condition. Rats were everywhere. The boy worked ten hours every day and didn't go to school. His name was Charles Dickens.

Dickens was born in Portsmouth in the south of England and later lived in Chatham in Kent and London when he was a child. He loved reading and enjoyed his school. However, when his family became poor, he had to work in the factory to help them. Luckily, his father was able to pay the money when his grandmother died and Charles stopped working and returned to school.

After he left school, Dickens worked in a law office and as a political journalist. His experiences in these jobs were important because he was able to use them later in his novels.

---

1.   **owed** : 欠 (錢)

Dickens in love

In 1830, Dickens fell in love for the first time. The girl's name was Maria Beadnell. But she came from a rich family and they didn't want her to marry a poor young man, so they sent her to school in Paris. Many years later, Dickens visited Maria again but found that she was rather fat and not very clever!

Dickens became successful and his first novel *The Pickwick Papers* was very popular. In 1836, he married Catherine Hogarth, the daughter of a newspaper editor. They had ten children. Catherine's sister, Mary, also lived with them.

By 1857 Dickens was a rich, world-famous writer and he met a young actress, Ellen Ternan. He was forty-five years old and she was eighteen. In 1858, he left his wife. People believe that Charles and Ellen fell in love and lived together for thirteen years but it was a secret. They even burnt the letters which they wrote to each other. After he died, Ellen received money from him for the rest of her life.

Crying for 'Little Nell'

Dickens published many of his stories week by week or month by month in magazines before they became books. He often tried to end a chapter with an exciting event, so that his readers wanted to buy the next magazine.

Mr Pickwick slides, from *The Pickwick Papers* (1837) by Charles Dickens, illustration by Hablot Knight Browne (known as Phiz).

After the success of *The Pickwick Papers*, he continued to write. Some of his early novels are *Oliver Twist, Nicholas Nickleby* and *The Old Curiosity Shop*. These aren't only good stories with interesting characters; they include social problems, such as **poverty**, education and the law.

In *The Old Curiosity Shop*, Little Nell, a young girl who is the heroine [1] of the novel, becomes ill. People wrote lots of letters to Dickens, asking him not to 'kill' her when he wrote the next part of the story in the next magazine. In the USA, people called to ships that arrived from England: 'Is Little Nell dead?' But Nell dies at the end of the story. Famous people said that when they read the story, they cried.

1. **a heroine** : 女主角

A world-famous writer

In 1843, Dickens published *A Christmas Carol*, the story of Ebenezer Scrooge, an old businessman who hates Christmas. He sees four ghosts who show him his mistakes, so he changes and becomes a **generous** man. Some of Dickens's later novels are *David Copperfield, Bleak House, Hard Times, Great Expectations* and *Our Mutual Friend*.

Dickens and his novels were popular all over the world. He travelled to the USA twice. On his first visit, in 1842, he gave talks in New York. There was a special dance for Dickens with 3,000 important people. However, the British writer wasn't happy with his experience of America. He hated **slavery**.

He visited America again in 1867-68 and read from his novels. This time, he thought that life in America was better. Dickens didn't only write novels. He also worked on magazines, gave talks, and worked with other writers. He was a very good actor and so he read from his novels in theatres. He worked very hard and perhaps this was bad for his health.

Scrooge's Third Visitor from *A Christmas Carol* (1843) by Charles Dickens, illustration by John Leech.

The train crash

On 9 June 1865, Dickens was returning from France by train with Ellen Ternan and her mother. The train crashed off a bridge at Staplehurst in Kent. Dickens helped the people who were hurt and went back to the train to get the papers of his new novel, *Our Mutual Friend*, which wasn't finished. Dickens didn't want anyone to know about Ellen, so he never talked about the crash.

Many people think that the experience of the train crash was a reason why Dickens's health became worse in the next few years. His doctors told him to rest but he didn't. Five years after the accident, on 9 June 1870, Charles Dickens died.

Dickens now

People love the novels of Dickens for many reasons. One is that he understood children and was able to describe their thoughts. He was sometimes sad when he was a child, so he created Oliver Twist with no family, David Copperfield, whose mother's second husband was cruel and Pip in *Great Expectations*, with a terrible sister who hits him.

Another reason is that the characters in his books have strange names like Ebenezer Scrooge, Mr Murdstone and Mr Pumblechook. They do strange things: for example, in *Great Expectations*, Miss Havisham lives for years in a house with no natural light and no clocks, still wearing her wedding dress.

Also, Dickens describes nineteenth-century London as a dirty, poor but interesting city and the society of the

Oliver amazed at the Dodger's mode of 'going to work', from *The Adventures of Oliver Twist* (1838) by Charles Dickens, illustration (1901) by George Cruikshank.

Dorset countryside, south of England.

Industrial revolution. We still use the word 'Dickensian' for anything that is like the conditions in England which he describes. The nineteenth century loved Dickens and so we do, too!

Thomas Hardy and 'Wessex'

Dickens used his imagination to create descriptions of London. Another novelist, Thomas Hardy, wrote about 'Wessex'. This wasn't a real place but it was like Dorset in the south of England, where Hardy lived. It was a place of farmers and workers, villages and small towns, natural beauty and sad love affairs.

Hardy's shocking[1] novels

Like Dickens, Hardy first published his novels in parts in magazines. Dickens's novels often have happy endings, but Hardy's novels usually end sadly. He thought that human life was often unhappy and that **fate** was **cruel**. He didn't like the social system of nineteenth-century Britain and showed that it was often bad for the ill or the poor. In his novel *Tess of the d'Urbervilles*, he told the story of a young woman, Tess, who has a baby when she is not married and later murders her lover. She is the heroine of the book, and many people didn't like this.

1.　**shocking** : 驚奇

In 1895, Hardy published *Jude the Obscure*. This is the story of Jude, a man who teaches himself and wants to go to Oxford University. He marries a girl from his village, Arabella, but then leaves her and falls in love with his cousin, Sue. Sue marries another man but leaves her husband to live with Jude. Their children die. It is a terrible, sad story. Hardy's wife, Emma, didn't like the book. In some shops, they sold *Jude the Obscure* secretly inside a paper bag. A bishop [1] burnt copies of the novel. Hardy stopped writing novels because a lot of people didn't understand or like them. He continued to write poetry, including a poem about the *Titanic*.

Hardy's life

Hardy was born in 1840 in Dorset. He studied to be an architect in London but then decided to be a writer. Some people think that he had a secret love affair with his cousin, Tryphena Sparks. In 1870, he met Emma Gifford, who became his first wife. They lived in a house called Max Gate. When Emma died in 1912, Hardy wrote many love poems about her. But he married again. What did his second wife, Florence Dugdale, think about these poems to his first wife?

In 1927, Thomas Hardy died. He wanted to be buried next to Emma in Dorset. His heart is buried there but because he was a great writer his body is in Poets' Corner in Westminster Abbey, in London. Dickens is also buried in Westminster Abbey, but he wanted to be buried near his home in Kent.

1.   **a bishop** : 主教

The text and **beyond**

ET **1** Comprehension check

Complete the following summary of the life of Charles Dickens. Write one word or date in each space.

Charles Dickens lived from (**1**) .... to (**2**) .... He was born in (**3**) .... but later lived in London and Chatham. When he was (**4**) .... years old, he had to work in a (**5**) .... because his (**6**) .... was in prison.

He wrote many novels; most of them were published in parts in (**7**) .... In (**8**) .... and 1867-68, he visited the (**9**) .... He married (**10**) .... in 1836 but when he met Ellen Ternan, a young (**11**) ...., he began a secret relationship with her. Nowadays, there are many films or TV dramas of his novels.

2 Thomas Hardy

What happened in Thomas Hardy's life in these years? Fill in the table. There is an example (**0**).

1840	Hardy was (**0**) ..born.. .
Before 1870	Perhaps he had a love affair with (**1**) ....
After 1870	He lived with his wife in a house called (**2**) ....
1895	He published (**3**) .... A bishop (**4**) .... copies of his novel.
1912	(**5**) .... died. He began to write (**6**) .... poems to her.
After 1912	He married (**7**) ....

5.1 ③ Listening

KET

You will hear some information about Rochester, one of the towns where Dickens lived.

Listen and complete questions 1-5. There is an example (0).

Dickens and Rochester

Rochester has an old (0) .....cathedral..... and a (1) ....

Dickens saw Gads Hill Place with his (2) .... when he was young. Later, he lived there.

In (3) .... *Expectations*, he wrote about the marshes [1].

Events and places to visit:

In (4) .... every year: the Dickens Festival

Dickens (5) ....

Before you read

① Vocabulary

Use a dictionary to check the meaning of words that you don't know in the box or table. Then add the words to the right group in the table.

aristocrat   private detective   Easter   senator   fascist

Group 1	Christmas	New Year	Valentine's Day	(1) ....
Group 2	spy	police officer	CIA agent	(2) ....
Group 3	(3)	lord	lady	duchess
Group 4	communist	socialist	anarchist	(4) ....
Group 5	king	(5)	prime minister	president

---

1.   **marshes** : 沼澤

CHAPTER SIX

Writers from Ireland

愛爾蘭聲音

Oscar Wilde
William Butler Yeats

Art for art's sake

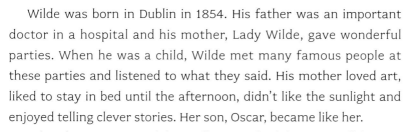

Many great writers were born in Ireland, such as Jonathan Swift, George Bernard Shaw, Sean O'Casey, James Joyce and Samuel Beckett. Ireland was a poor country, far from the centre of Europe, so many of them lived in Britain or other countries. Perhaps Oscar Wilde is the most famous. He wrote both for adults and children. He is famous for what he said and wrote.

Wilde was born in Dublin in 1854. His father was an important doctor in a hospital and his mother, Lady Wilde, gave wonderful parties. When he was a child, Wilde met many famous people at these parties and listened to what they said. His mother loved art, liked to stay in bed until the afternoon, didn't like the sunlight and enjoyed telling clever stories. Her son, Oscar, became like her.

When he was at Magdalen College, Oxford, he was well-known for being 'artistic'. He had long hair, wore fashionable clothes, didn't like sports, and had a lot of flowers and art in his room. Some other students didn't like this. They called him 'unmanly'

and once they threw him in the river. However, Wilde was part of an artistic fashion, 'aestheticism'. People used the name 'art for art's sake'. This means that art is important not because it is useful but because it is beautiful.

The marriage of a genius

Wilde wanted to marry Florence Balcombe. But she married Bram Stoker, the author of *Dracula*. When he knew this, Wilde moved from Dublin to London and said, 'I will never return to Ireland'.

At this time, Wilde needed money, so he went to the USA. When he entered the country, he said, 'I have nothing to declare [1] except my genius'. In America, he continued to shock the people. He wore strange clothes and talked about art and beauty.

In London, in 1884, he married Constance Lloyd. After an expensive wedding, they lived in a beautiful house and had two children. Wilde was the editor of a magazine, *Woman's World*, but he became more interested in writing stories and plays.

---

1. **I have nothing to declare** : 我沒有甚麼要申報

Wilde's success

Wilde wrote clever, funny stories like *Lord Arthur Savile's Crime* and *The Canterville Ghost*. In the first of these, Lord Arthur believes that he has to murder someone before he can get married. In the second, an American family meets an English ghost. He also wrote stories for children, like 'The Happy Prince' and 'The Selfish Giant'.

In 1890-91, Wilde published his only novel, *The Picture of Dorian Gray*. Dorian Gray is a beautiful young man who has a secret painting of himself. Dorian stays young but his image in the picture grows old. Dorian Gray takes opium and thinks that the most important thing in life is to enjoy himself. As a result, some people said that the book was 'unclean' and bad for its readers.

Wilde's plays also shocked some people. *Lady Windermere's Fan* and *An Ideal Husband* were both very popular but the stories included husbands and wives with secrets from each other. In 1895, at the St James's Theatre, London, Wilde's most successful play was performed, *The Importance of Being Earnest*. The play is one of the cleverest and funniest in the English language.

On the first night of the play, the Marquess of Queensbury, an

Funny cartoon showing Wilde's dream of an aesthetics future for America (1882) by Frederick Burr Opper.

Theatrical presentation (1942) of *The Importance of Being Earnest*.

English **aristocrat**, tried to enter the theatre. He was very angry with Wilde. They didn't let Queensbury come in, but this was the beginning of the unhappy part of Oscar Wilde's life.

Prison in England and a hotel in France

At this time in Britain, love between two men was against the law. The Marquess of Queensbury said that Oscar Wilde loved Queensbury's son, Lord Alfred Douglas. Wilde said that this was not true and used the law of libel [1] against Queensbury. But Queensbury used **private detectives** to get information. As a result, Wilde lost his law case and was found guilty of breaking the law. Wilde had time to leave England and go to France but he didn't and was arrested at the Cadogan Hotel in London.

He spent three years in prison. He was 'Prisoner C.C.3'. At first, they didn't even give him a pen and paper but later he was able

1. **libel** : 誹謗

to write. After he came out of prison, he published a poem about prison life, *The Ballad of Reading Gaol*. He also wanted better conditions in British prisons.

For the rest of his life, Wilde lived in France. His health was bad and he didn't write any more plays. He even used a different name, Sebastian Melmoth. He lived in the Hotel d'Alsace in Paris, away from his wife, children and most of his old friends. On 30 November 1900, Oscar Wilde died. He was buried in Paris; his **grave** is in the Père Lachaise cemetery.

Yeats and Irish nationalism

In the nineteenth century, Ireland was governed by the British. Many people in Ireland wanted to live in an independent country. These were the Irish nationalists. William Butler Yeats was interested in the idea of Ireland and Irish culture.

He was born in 1865 in Dublin but as a child he spent a lot of time in Sligo, a beautiful part of Ireland in the north-west. He called Sligo 'the country of the heart'. He loved old Irish stories and many of his poems talk about them. But Yeats's family was Protestant in religion, so he didn't always agree with the nationalists who wanted a Roman Catholic Ireland.

When he was a young man, Yeats wrote many beautiful poems about love and nature, such as *He Wishes for the Cloths of Heaven*, *When You Are Old* and *The Lake Isle of Innisfree*. They include many famous lines, for example:

When you are old and grey and full of sleep...

This was the kind of poetry of the 'Celtic Renaissance', the re-birth of Irish culture.

Later, Yeats's poems became less romantic and more political. In 1916, at **Easter**, some Irish nationalists in Dublin tried to fight the British army. This was known as 'The Easter Rising'. The

British won and the most important nationalists [1] died. Yeats wrote a poem about the Irish fighters who died. His poem 'Easter 1916' ends: 'A terrible beauty is born'. A few years later, the south of Ireland became independent.

In 1923, Yeats won the Nobel Prize for Literature. The Nobel judges said that his poems talked about 'the spirit of a whole nation'.

Yeats and Maude Gonne

In 1889, Yeats met Maude Gonne. She was 23 years old, beautiful, an actress and a strong Irish nationalist. Yeats fell in love with her, wrote poems about her and asked her to marry him many times during the next twenty-seven years! But he didn't agree with all her ideas about Ireland. So in 1903 Maude married Major John MacBride, a nationalist who later died in the Easter Rising. Yeats continued to love Maude. In 1916, he asked her for the last time to marry him. She said 'no'. A few months later, Yeats asked Maude's daughter, Iseult, to marry him. She also said 'no'. In October, 1916, Yeats married another woman, Georgie Hyde-Lees.

Another important woman in W. B. Yeats's life was his friend

---

1. **nationalists** : 民族主義者

Lissadel House in the County of Sligo, Ireland. Here Yeats wrote many of his famous plays and poems.

Lady Gregory. She asked him to write plays about Ireland and together they had the idea of an Irish theatre. In 1904, they opened the Abbey Theatre in Dublin. Maude Gonne performed in Yeats's first play there.

Yeats's ideas

After Ireland became independent, Yeats was a **senator** [1] in the new government for six years. For a time, he agreed with the ideas of Mussolini and the **fascists** [2] in Europe but his political ideas changed a lot during his life. One of his most famous poems, 'The Second Coming', seems to describe disorder in Europe and the rise of fascism. It was written in 1919-20. Some words from this poem — 'things fall apart' — were used by a Nigerian writer, Chinua Achebe, as the title for his 1958 novel about white Europeans arriving in Nigeria for the first time. These words were also the title of a hip-hop CD by The Roots in 1999.

He often talked on the radio. In one of his poems, he describes himself as a 'smiling public man'. When he was old, he continued to write about love. He is also one of the poets who writes best about old age.

Yeats died in France in 1939 at the age of seventy-three. He was buried first of all in France but later they moved his body to Ireland. This was what he wanted. He was buried in Sligo, Ireland, 'the country of the heart'.

1. **a senator**：参議員
2. **fascists**：法西斯主義者

The text and **beyond**

KET ① Comprehension check

Read the section 'Yeats and Maude Gonne' again. Are sentences 1-7 'Right' (A) or 'Wrong' (B)? If there is not enough information to answer A or B, choose 'Doesn't Say' (C). Write A, B or C in the space. There is an example (0).

0	Yeats and Maude Gonne met in 1889.	...A....
1	Maude Gonne was interested in Irish politics.	....
2	Yeats asked her to marry him ten times.	....
3	She married a man who had the same political ideas as she did.	....
4	Yeats married Maude Gonne's daughter.	....
5	Lady Gregory helped Yeats.	....
6	Irish plays were performed in England at the Abbey Theatre.	....
7	Maude Gonne was an excellent actress.	....

② 'The Selfish Giant'

Put sentences A-H in the right order to make a summary of part of the story 'The Selfish Giant' by Oscar Wilde. The first and last lines are already there.

A ☐ But next year, the spring didn't arrive in the giant's garden — it was always winter.

B ☐ He went away for seven years and the children played in his garden.

C ☐ The bird's song made him very happy and he looked out of his window.

D 8 Also, he saw that there were children everywhere.

E ☐ But one morning, when he woke up, he heard a bird singing.

F 1 There was a giant who had a beautiful garden.

G ☐ He saw that the trees had leaves and the sun shone.

H ☐ When the giant returned, he was very angry and he sent the children out.

T: GRADE 3

3 Speaking: places in the local area

Yeats loved Sligo, where he spent a lot of time when he was a child. Choose a place that you love and tell your partner about it. Use the following questions to ask him/her about his/her favourite place.

1 Where is the place?
2 What is it? (e.g. a city, a village, a park, a beach, a river, a mountain)
3 When do you go there? What do you do there? Who do you go there with?
4 When are you going to go there again?

Before you read

1 Vocabulary

You are going to read about Robert Louis Stevenson and Joseph Conrad. They sometimes wrote about dangerous people. Complete sentences 1-3 with words or phrases from the box. Use a dictionary if necessary.

Anarchists   Someone with a double personality   Violent people

1 .... like fighting and are often dangerous.
2 .... may sometimes be a good person and a bad person at other times.
3 .... want complete freedom. They don't want a government or any laws.

2 Find the words in the box in bold in Chapter Seven. What do you think that they mean? Write one word in each gap below.

colonies   Far East   sailor   voyages

In the nineteenth century, the British Empire was very powerful. There were British (**1**) .... in many places, including Africa, the Middle East and the (**2**) ....
Stevenson and Conrad both loved the sea. Stevenson went on many (**3**) .... in the Pacific and finally lived on an island in Samoa. Joseph Conrad was a (**4**) .... for many years.

CHAPTER SEVEN

Travellers

歷奇精神

Robert Louis Stevenson
Joseph Conrad

Health problems

Robert Louis Stevenson was born in Edinburgh in 1850. His father
and grandfather were lighthouse [1] engineers and they wanted
Robert to do the same work. He was a clever child but had bad
health. His nurse, Alison Cunningham (he called her 'Cummie'),
read him lots of stories. Perhaps that is why he loved books. At
university, he studied engineering and then law. Stevenson wanted
to be a writer but his father didn't understand this.

Because he had bad health, his doctors told him to live
in warm countries and not to stay in Scotland in the winter.
Stevenson was pleased because he loved travelling. After
university, he spent four years in France. He travelled a lot and
he wrote about one special trip with a donkey [2] called Modestine:
this book is called *Travels with a Donkey*.

1. **a lighthouse** : 燈塔
2. **a donkey** : 驢

A great love story

In 1876, Stevenson found a new reason to travel. This was when he met Fanny Vandegrift Osbourne in France. She was an American woman, ten years older than him and unhappily married. When she returned to San Francisco Stevenson followed her, but he didn't tell his father. He travelled to New York and then to California, where he lived on forty-five cents a day and tried to earn money by writing. He

became very ill and almost died. Fanny was now divorced and she looked after him until he was well again. They married in 1880. Finally, Robert returned home to Britain. He lived with his wife in the south of England and in France because of his bad health.

Map of Treasure Island in a 1883 edition of the book.

The art of words

Stevenson said that he loved 'the art of words'. In 1881, he made a map for Fanny's son, Lloyd. As he looked at the map, he began to imagine the story of *Treasure Island*. In 1884, he had a strange dream. In this dream, a man got away from the police by changing into another person. This gave him the idea for the famous short novel *The Strange Case of Dr Jekyll and Mr Hyde* about a man who has a **double personality**, one good and the other bad.

Villa Vailima, Robert Louis Stevenson's home in Samoa.

'To travel hopefully is a better thing than to arrive' [1]

When his father died in 1887, Stevenson decided to travel again. He loved the sea and he loved new places. He went with his family and his mother to America and then visited the South Pacific Ocean on a sailing boat with his family.

He made two more **voyages** to the South Pacific in 1889 and 1890. Finally, he bought some land on an island in Samoa in the South Pacific and built a house. He enjoyed helping the Samoan people and didn't like the Europeans who controlled them. The Samoans called him 'Tusitala', which means 'story-teller'.

He began to write a new novel, *Weir of Hermiston,* but he never finished it. On 3 December 1894, he suddenly said to his wife 'What's that!' and then fell to the floor. A few hours later he died. The Samoan people buried him in a place where you could see the sea. On his grave, they wrote one of his poems, which begins: 'Under the wide and starry sky, dig the grave and let me lie'.

---

1. **'to travel hopefully is a better thing than to arrive'**：滿懷希望去旅行比到達目的地更暢快

Heart of Darkness

Stevenson looked at both the good and bad parts of people. But the most famous story by Joseph Conrad is *Heart of Darkness* about the terrible things that human beings can do. The character who tells the story, Marlow, travels up the Congo river in Africa to find an unusual European, Kurz.

Kurz is a cruel man who lives in the middle of the African forest. The heads of people that he killed are all around his house. When Marlow finds him, he is dying and his last words are 'The horror! The horror!' Marlow visits Kurz's fiancée in Europe, who believes that he was a good man. He doesn't tell her the truth but says that Kurz said her name when he died.

Conrad lived in the time when some European countries had empires. Many European countries had **colonies** in parts of Asia and Africa. In *Heart of Darkness*, perhaps Conrad wants to say that at the heart of the empire there is **violence** and love of money but people in Europe think that the empire is good.

A dangerous start to life

Joseph Conrad was a very interesting man. He was Polish and was born in the Ukraine in 1857. His real name was Jozef Teodor Konrad Korzeniowski. He spoke Polish and French but only learnt English when he was more than twenty years old. In 1861, his father, Apollo Korzeniowski, was arrested by the Russians for political reasons. He, his wife and four-year-old Jozef were sent to a cold, unpleasant part of Russia.

View of the Congo river.

After the family returned to the Ukraine, both his mother and father died. Jozef lived with his uncle until he was sixteen. The Russians wanted him in their army but he went to France and became a **sailor** instead.

Conrad's voyages

Conrad was a sailor from the age of sixteen to thirty-six. He had many adventures. He took guns secretly by sea from one country to another; he visited Mauritius and fell in love with a Mauritian woman, Eugenie, who didn't want to marry him; he lost a lot of money by gambling [1] and tried to kill himself.

In 1878, he worked on a British ship and visited England for the first time. There, he began to learn English. He travelled all over the world on British ships, including South America, India,

1. **gambling** : 賭博

Australia, South East Asia and the **Far East**. These voyages gave him things to write about in his novels. In 1889, he went to Africa and worked as the captain of a small ship on the Congo river. The terrible things that he saw there gave him the idea for *Heart of Darkness*.

In 1886, Jozef became Joseph Conrad, a British citizen. He married an English wife and died in 1924 near Canterbury, Kent. By this time, he was a famous British writer but his Polish name is written on his grave.

Stories from all over the world

After he left the navy, Conrad wrote many novels in English. English was his third language but Conrad soon became famous as a writer. *Nostromo* is a story about South America and a treasure of silver; *Lord Jim* is about a British sailor living in Indonesia, *The Secret Agent* is about an **anarchist** in London.

His readers enjoyed his books because the stories take place in exciting, foreign places. However, Conrad had a negative view of human beings. His characters don't live perfect lives. They are often only interested in money or are violent or think only about themselves. Conrad had a hard, dangerous early life and his books show this.

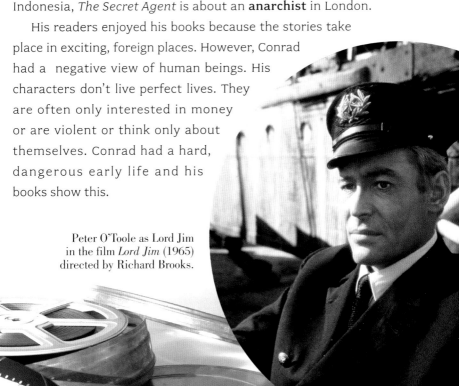

Peter O'Toole as Lord Jim in the film *Lord Jim* (1965) directed by Richard Brooks.

The text and **beyond**

1 Comprehension check

Answer the following questions about Chapter Seven.

1 Why did Stevenson travel to America?
2 Which countries did he and his wife live in?
3 Where was he buried?
4 Where is *Heart of Darkness* set?
5 How old was Conrad when he started learning English?
6 Where did he meet a woman who didn't want to marry him?

KET 2 Vocabulary

Read the descriptions 1-5 of some jobs in Chapter Seven. The first letter is already there. There is one space for each other letter in the word.

1 I work on ships and travel on the sea.   s _ _ _ _ _
2 I look after sick people or children.   n _ _ _ _
3 People enjoy reading my stories.   w _ _ _ _ _
4 I help sick people and give them medicine.   d _ _ _ _ _
5 I am the most important person on a ship.   c _ _ _ _ _ _

T: GRADE 4

3 Speaking: work

Stevenson did different kinds of work and Conrad was a sailor. What work does someone in your family or a friend do? Talk to a partner about the job. Use questions 1-4 to help you.

1 What is the person's job?
2 What does the person do in his/her job?
3 How much time does he/she work and where does he/she work?
4 Does the person like the job?

④ Prepositions 介詞

Here are some sentences from Chapter Seven. Don't look back at the chapter. Complete the sentences with a preposition.

1 He spent four years .... France.

2 A man got away .... the police.

3 His father died .... 1887.

4 They were sent .... Russia from the Ukraine.

5 Jozef lived .... his uncle until he was sixteen.

6 *Nostromo* is a story .... South America.

⑤ Listening

Listen to Sally talking to Josh about Stevenson and Conrad. For questions 1-5, underline the correct words to complete the sentences. There is an example (0).

0 Sally saw **a film**/**a play**/**the news** on TV last night.

1 When Josh was a child, he **didn't read**/**liked**/**didn't finish** *Treasure Island*.

2 Stevenson wrote the book about **113**/**130**/**100** years ago.

3 Josh and Sally **agree**/**are not sure**/**don't agree** that *Treasure Island* is only for boys.

4 *Apocalypse Now* is **a film from the 70s**/**a film from Vietnam**/**a film by Conrad**.

5 Josh **likes**/**didn't know about**/**wants to see** *Apocalypse Now*.

Joseph Fiennes in a scene from John Madden's
film *Shakespeare in Love* (1998).

Writers and Films

名著搬上銀幕

There are hundreds of films of novels and plays by British authors or about their lives. Here is some information about three of the best.

Shakespeare in Love

There are many films of Shakespeare's plays with famous actors but one of the most successful, Oscar-winning films is about Shakespeare himself. John Madden directed *Shakespeare in Love* in 1998. It stars Joseph Fiennes as Shakespeare and Gwyneth Paltrow as Viola, the young woman who loves him.

The film doesn't show us the true life of Shakespeare. For example it includes some 21st century language! It is a very funny film but also shows us a very unhappy love story between Shakespeare and Viola de Lesseps. Shakespeare has no money and Viola is the daughter of a rich family. She has to marry a lord (played by Colin Firth) but Queen Elizabeth (Judi Dench) helps the lovers.

The film helps us to understand Shakespeare and his plays. It shows us the wooden theatre where he worked and the type of people that watched the plays. It also shows us the problems for the theatre in Shakespeare's time – with no girls in the theatre and no modern technology. There is even a fight between two theatre companies.

Pride and Prejudice

Pride and Prejudice is Jane Austen's most popular novel and there are many adaptations [1] of it for the TV and for the cinema. The most recent film was made in 2005. A very successful TV series of the book was made in the 1990s, so it was difficult for the director, Joe Wright, to follow it with a successful film. Most people think that both the TV series and the film are excellent.

Pride and Prejudice is about two young people, Elizabeth Bennet and Mr Darcy. Darcy is very proud and at first Elizabeth doesn't like him – he suffers from 'pride' and she suffers from 'prejudice'. In the film, Matthew Macfadyen plays Darcy and Keira Knightley plays Elizabeth. You can see how people lived in the early nineteenth century, the clothes that they wore and the way they spent their time. The film did

1. **adaptations** : 改編

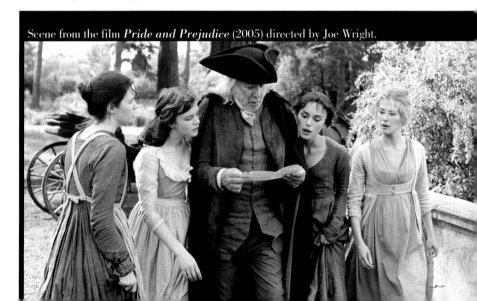

Scene from the film *Pride and Prejudice* (2005) directed by Joe Wright.

not win an Oscar but it earned 121 million US dollars in cinemas all over the world.

Great Expectations

A young child is near the church in the countryside. He is alone and looking at the grave of his dead parents. Suddenly a big man appears and catches him.

Later, the child goes to the house of a rich old lady. She sits in a room with no natural light wearing a yellow wedding dress. None of the clocks in her house is moving. Her only companion is a beautiful young girl, Estella.

These are two moments from the film of *Great Expectations*. In 1946, a young British film director, David Lean, made the film in black and white. David Lean later made many Oscar-winning films – *Lawrence of Arabia*, *Doctor Zhivago (1965),* – and *Great Expectations* is very good too.

Scene from the film *Great Expectations* (1946) directed by David Lean.

Scene from the film *Great Expectations* (1998) directed by Alfonso Cuarón.

There are other films of Dickens's story. In 1997, the director Alfonso Cuarón moved the story to New York and made a modern version about an artist with Ethan Hawke, Gwyneth Paltrow and Robert De Niro.

1 Comprehension check

Complete this fact file.

Film title	Date	Director	Author of original book/play	Main actors	Oscars
Shakespeare in Love	(1)	(2)	—	(3) .... and (4)	yes
Pride and Prejudice	(5)	(6)	(7)	(8) .... and (9)	no
Great Expectations	1946	(10)	(11)	—	no
Great Expectations	(12)	(13)	—	(14) .... (15) .... (16)	no

Before you read

1 Vocabulary

In Chapter Eight you will read about writers who wrote some political novels. Look at the sentences A-E and then match them to the different political ideas 1-5. Use a dictionary to help you.

	noun — the idea	noun — the person	sentence
1	communism	a communist	
2	fascism	a fascist	
3	socialism	a socialist	
4	Stalinism	a Stalinist	
5	a dictatorship	a dictator	

A 'I want to build better schools and hospitals for the workers.'

B 'Stalin is a great leader. His ideas are the best!'

C 'I am the best leader. Do everything that I want!'

D 'The people are important. Everyone must have the same.'

E 'We need a strong leader. Our country is great!'

2 Complete the words in 1-5. You can find the answers in bold in Chapter Eight.

1 These people ask for money in the street.   b _ _ _ _ _

2 These people take money which is not theirs.   t _ _ _ _ _

3 This person has no home but travels on foot from place to place.   t _ _ _ _

4 The police want to catch this person.   c _ _ _ _ _ _ _

5 These are places where poor people can sleep.   h _ _ _ _ _

Twentieth-Century Writers

反映時弊

George Orwell
Graham Greene

After the First World War (1914-1918), there were a lot of changes in Europe. **Fascism** became important in Germany and Italy and Stalinism in Russia. At the same time, many people asked questions about the European colonies in Africa and Asia. Should these countries be independent? George Orwell wrote in these political conditions.

An honest writer

George Orwell wasn't his real name. Eric Blair was born in India in 1903 but came to England with his parents when he was one. For part of his school life he went to Eton College. But his exam results were bad and his parents decided to send Eric to Burma, part of the British Empire in Asia, to become a policeman.

Eric Blair liked the Burmese people but he didn't like the way that the British considered them. One time, he had to shoot a dangerous elephant: he wrote about this in 'Shooting an Elephant'.

He spent five years in Burma and then decided to return to Europe.

In Europe, Blair wanted to experience the life of poor people. In Paris, he washed the dirty dishes in restaurants. He had very little money and lived in bad conditions. When he returned to England, he decided to become a **tramp** [1]. He met **beggars** and **thieves** and slept in **hostels** [2] for the poor. He wrote about these experiences in *Down and Out in Paris and London*. He didn't use his real name on this book. Instead, he chose the name 'George Orwell'.

Orwell wrote about the things that he experienced, honestly and clearly, and helped his readers to understand other people's lives.

In 1936, there was a civil war in Spain, where Hitler's Germany was helping General Franco fight the republicans. Orwell wanted to help the Spanish people by fighting against Hitler and Franco. He went to Barcelona and took part in the war. When he was shot in the neck, he nearly died. His book *Homage to Catalonia* is a wonderful record of the war.

The world of Big Brother

When Orwell wrote *Animal Farm*, he became famous. It tells the story of some animals who take control of a farm from the human farmers. Little by little, the pigs take control over the other animals. Orwell's readers knew that he was really writing about Stalinism in Russia. The 'pigs' were the **communists**. Orwell was a true **socialist** but he didn't like Russian communism because Stalin controlled the people and killed people who didn't agree with him.

In 1948, Orwell published *1984*. This is a book about the future. He imagined a

1. **a tramp** : 流浪者
2. **hostels** : 收容所

Scene from the film *Nineteen Eighty-Four* (1984) directed by Michael Radford.

world where people had no freedom; the government controlled everything. Orwell gave the name 'Big Brother' to the **dictator** who watches everything using technology. Now it is the name of a TV programme and we also use it for any society where people are watched by the government.

'Greeneland'

Graham Greene was born in 1904. Like Orwell, he was interested in politics but he was also interested in religion. For most of his life he was a Roman Catholic.

Greene's father was headmaster [1] at his school and the other boys were very unkind to him because of it. Greene hated this and even tried to kill himself. He went to Oxford University and then worked as a journalist. In 1927, he married his wife, Vivien, who was also a strong Catholic. Later in his life, he lived with other women but he never got divorced from Vivien.

In 1937-1938, Greene went to Mexico and later wrote *The Power and the Glory* about a Catholic priest in Mexico. Some Roman Catholics didn't like the book but the Pope, Paul VI, told Greene that the novel was good. He often wrote stories about people in poor,

---

1. **a headmaster** : 校長

Scene from the film *The Third Man* (1949)
directed by Carol Reed.

hot countries like Cuba, Vietnam, Argentina, Haiti and West Africa.
People called the people and places in his books 'Greeneland'.

Greene said that he wrote two types of books. He wrote
'entertainments' — exciting, popular stories — to earn money.
But other books were about more important subjects, like *The
Power and the Glory*. In fact, many of his 'entertainments' are
very well-written novels.

He also wrote plays and screenplays[1] for films: the most famous
film is *The Third Man* about a **criminal** in Vienna after the Second
World War. Many of his novels have become films, including
Brighton Rock about a small criminal in an English town by the sea.
People thought that he should win a Nobel Prize but he never did.

Spy and secret lover

His sister, Elisabeth, worked for the British secret service and
during the Second World War, Greene became a spy for MI6.
Some people think that he was a spy for the rest of his life.

1. **a screenplay** : 劇本

During the war, he worked with a man called Kim Philby and became his friend. Later, it was clear that Philby was a double agent who worked for the Russians. After Philby went to Russia, Greene visited him in Moscow. We know that Greene continued to give information to the British government until he died.

Greene spent a lot of time travelling. He knew Fidel Castro, the President of Cuba, and 'Papa Doc', the dictator in Haiti. He didn't like United States policy and during the Vietnam War[1] he wrote *The Quiet American*. This novel showed Greene's idea that American policy in Vietnam was bad.

In 1966, Greene left Britain and went to Antibes in the South of France to live with Yvonne Cloetta, a French woman who was his lover for thirty-two years. He wanted to keep their love affair secret but in the end people knew about it. In France, Greene wrote that the city government of Nice worked with criminals. This wasn't true, said the people, but later it was clear that Greene was right.

Greene then moved to Vevey on Lake Geneva in Switzerland. He became friends with Charlie Chaplin there and wrote one of his last novels, *Doctor Fischer of Geneva*. In 1991, he died at the age of 86.

After Orwell and Greene, there were and still are many good writers in Britain. Some, like William Golding, Harold Pinter, Doris Lessing and Seamus Heaney, an Irish poet, won the Nobel Prize for Literature. Some were born in other countries, like Salman Rushdie, but lived and wrote in Britain. People continue to write important novels, plays and poetry in Britain.

1. **the Vietnam War**：越南戰爭

The text and **beyond**

1 Comprehension check

Complete these facts about George Orwell and Graham Greene. Write no more than three words or a date in each gap.

George Orwell

1 His real name was ....

2 He was born at the beginning of the .... century.

3 His first job was as a .... in Burma.

4 He wrote a book about his experiences when he did dirty jobs and lived with poor people in .... and London.

5 He fought in the .... Civil War.

6 His two most famous books are .... and ....

Graham Greene

7 Religion was important for Greene. He was a ....

8 He never got .... from his wife but they separated.

9 Greene called his less important books '.....................' .

10 He wrote the film ....

11 He never won the ....

12 He was a .... in the second World War.

KET 2 Vocabulary

Read the descriptions 1-5 of some people in Chapter Eight. The first letter is already there. There is one space for each other letter in the word.

1 I am a famous actor or actress in a film. s _ _ _

2 We have got one or more children. p _ _ _ _ _

3 I want to arrest number 2. p _ _ _ _ _ _ _

4 Books, magazines, newspapers, etc. are for me! r _ _ _ _ _

5 I am a good person. I am the most important person in a story. h _ _ _

3 Who was it?

Complete 1-9 by writing the names of writers from the box.

> Mary Anne Evans   Ben Jonson   Christopher Marlowe
> John Milton (x 2)   George Orwell   Alexander Pope
> Robert Louis Stevenson   W. B. Yeats

1   Graham Greene was a spy. Another writer who was probably a spy was ....

2   Greene travelled to many countries. Another writer who loved travelling was ....

3   Greene did not divorce his wife. But a poet who wrote about divorce was ....

4   Greene did not win a Nobel Prize. .... won a Nobel Prize.

5   Greene was interested in politics. .... was also interested in politics.

6   Greene was a Roman Catholic. .... was also a Catholic.

7   Eric Blair changed his name when he wrote. .... was another writer who did this.

8   Orwell was in a war. .... was a soldier in the Netherlands.

9   Orwell was in a Civil War. .... lived when there was a Civil War.

4 Discussion

In Chapter Eight you read about Big Brother in Orwell's book *Nineteen Eighty-Four*. Why is the name 'Big Brother' famous now in the 21st century? How can governments control what people do? Do you think that the people in your country are 'watched' by the government?

1 **Great British Writers Quiz**

A Answer these questions about the writers in this book. You get one point for each correct answer.

Total points:

30-40 = excellent   25-29 = very good   20-24 = good

Section One: books, plays and poems

Who wrote:

1 *Paradise Lost*?

2 'Kubla Khan'?

3 *Doctor Faustus*?

4 *The Picture of Dorian Gray*?

5 *Down and Out in Paris and London*?

6 154 sonnets?

7 *Wuthering Heights*?

8 *Middlemarch*?

Section Two: births and deaths

1 Where did Byron die?

2 On what date in 1616 did Shakespeare die?

3 Which writer was Polish?

4 Who is buried in Sligo in Ireland?

5 Where is Keats buried?

6 Which writer died after she went to her brother's funeral?

7 Who is buried in Winchester cathedral?

8 The heart of which writer is buried in Dorset?

Section Three: love and marriage

1 Who was Fanny Brawne?

2 Who wrote poems to a 'dark lady'?

3 Who was 'mad, bad, and dangerous to know'?

4 Who was in a train accident with an actress and her mother?

5   Which poet was married three times?

6   Which writer's wife did not like his novel *Jude the Obscure*?

7   Which writer wrote about love but never married?

8   Who followed the woman that he loved to America?

Section Four: lives

1   Which war did Orwell take part in?

2   Who walked from London to Scotland?

3   Who lived with George Henry Lewes without getting married?

4   Who was Eric Blair?

5   Who were Acton Bell, Currer Bell and Ellis Bell?

6   Which writer was only 1.37 metres tall?

7   The Russians arrested his father. Which writer is this?

8   Who wrote the screenplay for the film *The Third Man*?

Section Five: places

1   Who was in prison in Reading?

2   Her husband jumped into the Grand Canal in Venice. Which writer is this?

3   Who wrote about 'Wessex'?

4   Who lived at Haworth in the north of England?

5   Who was killed in an inn near the Thames?

6   Who moved outside London because his family were Roman Catholic?

7   Where did Dickens work when he was twelve years old?

8   In which city did the 'Easter Rising' happen?

B   **Write ten more quiz questions about writers in this book. Use information from the eight chapters and the dossiers. Then ask other students to answer them.**

Black Cat Discovery 閱讀系列：

London
倫敦今昔

Gina D. B. Clemen

audio｜mp3

Discovery

1
Level

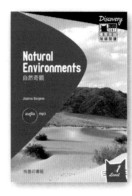

Natural Environments
自然奇觀

Joanna Burgess

商務印書館

Discovery

1
Level

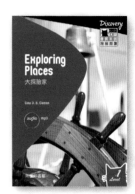

Exploring Places
大探險家

Gina D. B. Clemen

audio｜mp3

Discovery

1
Level

American Cities
美國都會

Gina D. B. Clemen

audio｜mp3

商務印書館

Discovery

2
Level

The British Isles
英倫諸島

Derek Sellen

audio｜mp3

商務印書館

Discovery

2
Level

The English-speaking World
英語世界

Janet Cameron

audio｜mp3

商務印書館

Discovery

2
Level

Great British Writers
英國著名作家

Derek Sellen

audio｜mp3

商務印書館

Discovery

1
Level

Level 1 ana